Catch That Chicken!

Atinuke
illustrated by Angela Brooksbank

For Mara Menzies and Imani Sykes, who first thought of a chicken chaser!
And for Lani-Grace, who is one! ~ A.

For my mother, known as Granny Chicken, because she loves chickens! ~ A.B.

Notes: This story takes place in West Africa. *Sannu* means "take it easy."

Text copyright © 2020 by Atinuke ✪ Illustrations copyright © 2020 by Angela Brooksbank ✪ All rights reserved. No part of this book may be reproduced, transmitted, or stored in an information retrieval system in any form or by any means, graphic, electronic, or mechanical, including photocopying, taping, and recording, without prior written permission from the publisher. ✪ First U.S. edition 2020 ✪ Library of Congress Catalog Card Number pending ✪ ISBN 978-1-5362-1268-6 ✪ This book was typeset in Schinn Medium ✪ The illustrations were done in mixed media ✪ Candlewick Press, 99 Dover Street, Somerville, Massachusetts 02144 ✪ visit us at www.candlewick.com ✪ Printed in Shenzhen, Guangdong, China ✪
20 21 22 23 24 25 CCP 10 9 8 7 6 5 4 3 2 1

CANDLEWICK PRESS

This is Lami.

Lami loves chickens.
Luckily, Lami lives
in a compound . . .

with lots and lots of chickens.

"Catch 'am, Lami! Catch 'am!"
shouts brother Bilal.

"Catch that chicken!"
shouts Nana Nadia.

"Catch that chicken!"
shouts friend Fatima.

"Catch 'am, Lami! Catch 'am!"
shouts sister Sadia.

"Catch 'am, Lami! Catch 'am!"

"Catch that chicken!"
shouts Daddy Danlami.

"Catch that chicken!"
shouts Aunty Aisha.

Lami leans!

Lami lunges!

Lami leaps!

And Lami
catches her!

Lami is the **best** chicken catcher in the village.

Sister Sadia is speedy
at spelling.
But when it comes
to chickens . . .

Lami is
speedier.

Friend Fatima is fast
at braiding hair.

But when it comes
to chickens . . .

Lami is faster.

Big brother Bilal
is brave with bulls.

But when it comes
to chickens . . .

Lami is braver.

One day Lami chases a chicken through the pen.

"Sannu! Sannu!"
shout the uncles.

"Slow down!"

She chases that chicken around the compound.

"Sannu! Sannu!" shout the aunties.

"SLOW DOWN!"

She chases that chicken up
the big baobab.

"Sannu! Sannu!"
shout the elders.

"SLOW DOWN!"

But Lami scrambles speedily.

Lami snatches suddenly.

Lami slips swiftly.

And
she falls!

She sprains her ankle

so badly it puffs up like the neck

of an angry lizard.

Lami cries.

It hurts and now she can't chase,

she can't climb,

and she definitely can't

catch chickens.

"If you are not careful,

you will soon be best in the village at crying,"

says Nana Nadia with a smile.

"It's not quick feet that catches chickens —

it's quick thinking."

Lami stares at her.

And Lami thinks.

She thinks slowly . . .

and then she thinks *quickly* . . .

and suddenly Lami knows

exactly what to do!

She can make the chickens come right to her!

"Catch that chicken!"
whispers Nana Nadia.

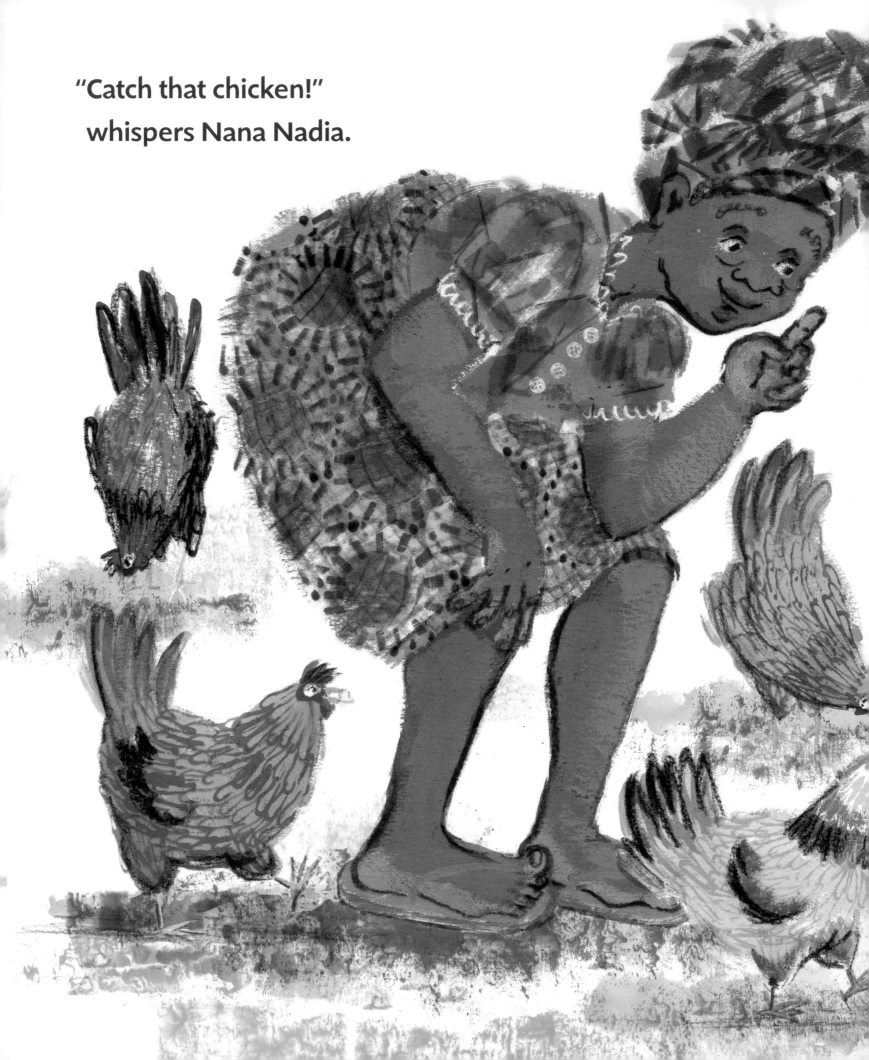

"Caught her!"
says Lami.

She is still the **best** chicken catcher in the village.

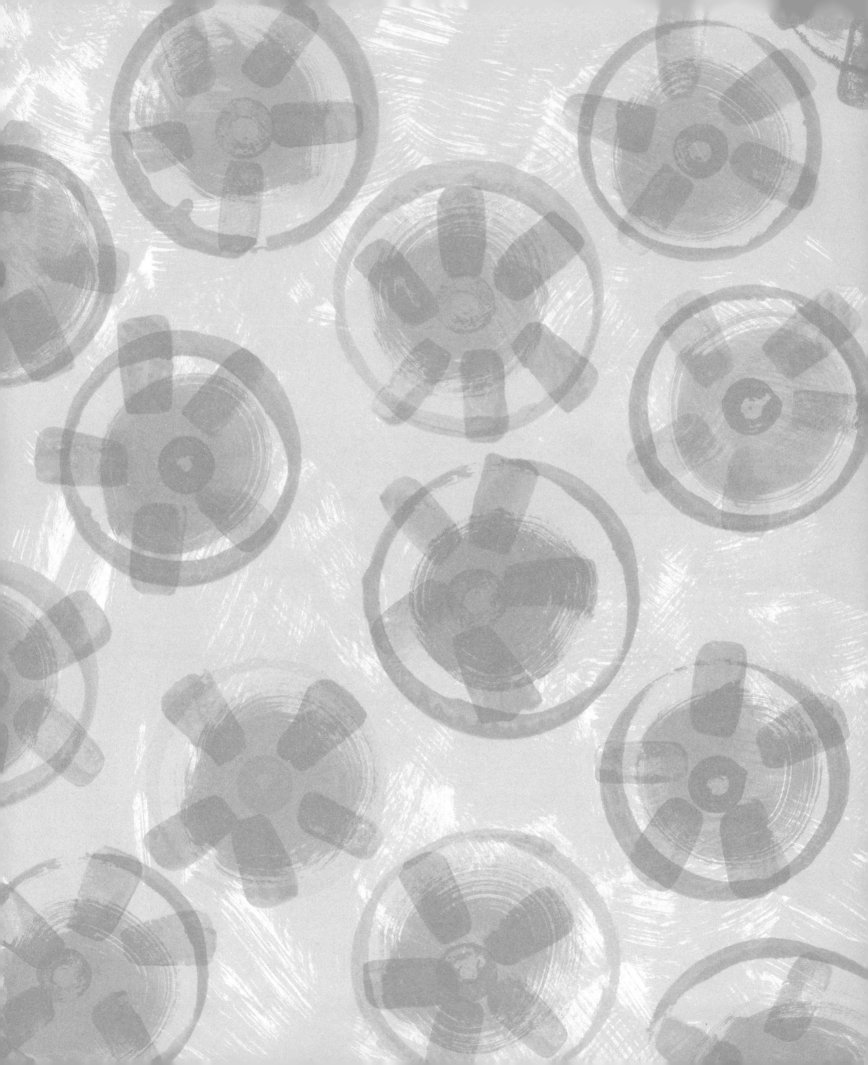